★ *For Lily John, who showed me her fairy letters,*
and for Josie, just because ★ *A. D.*

★ *For Helena, Denise, and Julie,*
thank you all ★ *V. C.*

First U.S. edition 2004

Library of Congress Cataloging-in-Publication Data is available.

Library of Congress Catalog Card Number 2003040944

ISBN 0-7636-2175-7

10 9 8 7 6 5 4 3 2 1

Printed in China

This book was typeset in Palatino. The illustrations were done in watercolor and pencil.

Candlewick Press, 2067 Massachusetts Avenue, Cambridge, Massachusetts 02140

visit us at www.candlewick.com

CANDLEWICK PRESS
CAMBRIDGE, MASSACHUSETTS

Dear Tooth Fairy

Alan Durant

illustrated by
Vanessa Cabban

Holly's tooth was loose. It got looser
and looser . . . and then it fell out!
I could give it to the Tooth Fairy, she thought,
and get a coin. But Holly liked her tooth
and wanted to keep it. So she put some plastic
vampire fangs under her pillow instead.

"The Tooth Fairy should be happy because
she's getting *lots* of teeth," Holly said.

The next morning the vampire fangs were
still there. But there was a tiny envelope too.

HOLLY

Holly read the Tooth Fairy's note over and over. She was delighted.

I will write back, she thought. This is what she wrote:

Dear Tooth Fairy,

Thank you for coming last night. I've never had a visit from the Tooth Fairy before.

I have a few questions.

Why do you want my tooth?

How did you know it had come out?

Are there lots of tooth fairies or are you the only one?

Where do you live?

Please answer.

Love, Holly

P.S. I drew a picture of you.

I hope you like it.

Holly put the letter under her pillow.

That night the Tooth Fairy came back.

When Holly looked under her pillow
the next morning, her note was gone.
In its place was a new envelope.

Holly read the letter and looked
at the leaflet. She thought
about tooth fairies,
flying hither and thither
around the world.

All that day Holly wondered what
Fairyland must be like.
She wrote another note
to the Tooth Fairy.

Dear Tooth Fairy,
Thank you so much for your letter.
I'm glad you liked my picture, but
(please don't be angry!) there's
just one more thing I need to know
(well, two things actually).
Are there different kinds of fairies?
What do they do all day and night?
I know the fairies want my tooth, but I want
to be sure they will be good owners.
Love,
Holly

That night the Tooth Fairy
visited once more.

Holly read the letter and studied her poster. She liked it very much. She wanted to help the Tooth Fairy, but she still wasn't sure about giving up her tooth. Then she had an idea.

Dear Tooth Fairy,

Thank you for the poster. It's beautiful.

I think all the fairies are wonderful, but I like tooth fairies the best.

Do you like riddles? I do! Here's a challenge for you. If you ask me a riddle that I can't answer, I'll give you my tooth.

That's fair, isn't it? By the way, I know one of those boggarts— my little brother!

Love, Holly

Holly loved her fairy riddle-teller. It was the best present she'd ever received. She knew that now was the time to give the Tooth Fairy a present too. That evening Holly put her tooth under her pillow.

"Goodbye, tooth," she said. And she left a final note for the Tooth Fairy.

Dear Tooth Fairy,
The answer to your riddle is they both have roots. But don't worry. I'm giving you my tooth anyway because I know how much you need it.
I hope the Fairy Queen likes her new throne!
Thank you very much for visiting me and being so patient.
I hope to hear from you again sometime.
Goodbye!
Lots of love, Holly ×××

That night, the Tooth Fairy
came for the last time.
She took Holly's tooth and left
a letter. Then she flew back
to Fairyland.

When she got there, she
put the tooth in its place
on the Fairy Queen's
new throne.

The next morning Holly read
the letter and smiled at her new
coin. She thought about the
Tooth Fairy and hoped that
       she'd come again soon.

In fact . . . yes,
one of Holly's teeth
was definitely loose. . . .

It was time to start
another letter to the
Tooth Fairy!